THE GRUFFALO

Julia Donaldson

Illustrated by Axel Scheffler

MACMILLAN CHILDREN'S BOOKS

A mouse took a stroll through the deep dark wood.
A fox saw the mouse and the mouse looked good.
"Where are you going to, little brown mouse?
Come and have lunch in my underground house."
"It's terribly kind of you, Fox, but no —
I'm going to have lunch with a gruffalo."

"A gruffalo? What's a gruffalo?"
"A gruffalo! Why, didn't you know?

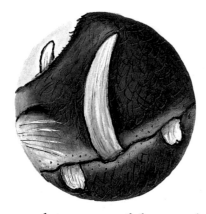

"He has terrible tusks,   and terrible claws,

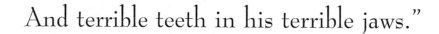

And terrible teeth in his terrible jaws."

"*Where are you meeting him?*"
"Here, by these rocks,
And his favourite food is roasted fox."

"Roasted fox! I'm off!" Fox said.
"Goodbye, little mouse," and away he sped.

"Silly old Fox! Doesn't he know,
There's no such thing as a gruffalo?"

On went the mouse through the deep dark wood.
An owl saw the mouse and the mouse looked good.
"*Where are you going to, little brown mouse?*
Come and have tea in my treetop house."
"It's frightfully nice of you, Owl, but no —
I'm going to have tea with a gruffalo."

"*A gruffalo? What's a gruffalo?*"
"A gruffalo! Why, didn't you know?

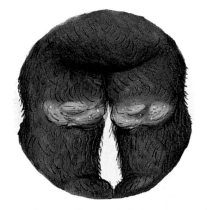 

"He has knobbly knees,   and turned-out toes,

And a poisonous wart at the end of his nose."

"*Where are you meeting him?*"
"Here, by this stream,
And his favourite food is owl ice cream."

"Owl ice cream? Toowhit toowhoo!
Goodbye, little mouse," and away Owl flew.

"Silly old Owl! Doesn't he know,
There's no such thing as a gruffalo?"

On went the mouse through the deep dark wood.
A snake saw the mouse and the mouse looked good.
"*Where are you going to, little brown mouse?*
Come for a feast in my logpile house."
"It's wonderfully good of you, Snake, but no —
I'm having a feast with a gruffalo."

"*A gruffalo? What's a gruffalo?*"
"A gruffalo! Why, didn't you know?

"His eyes are orange,   his tongue is black;

He has purple prickles all over his back."

"Where are you meeting him?"
"Here, by this lake,
And his favourite food is scrambled snake."

"Scrambled snake! It's time I hid!
Goodbye, little mouse," and away Snake slid.

"Silly old Snake! Doesn't he know,
There's no such thing as a gruffal . . .

. . . Oh!"

But who is this creature with terrible claws
And terrible teeth in his terrible jaws?
He has knobbly knees and turned-out toes
And a poisonous wart at the end of his nose.
His eyes are orange, his tongue is black;
He has purple prickles all over his back.

"Oh help! Oh no!
It's a gruffalo!"

"*My favourite food!*" the Gruffalo said.
"*You'll taste good on a slice of bread!*"

"Good?" said the mouse. "Don't call me good!
I'm the scariest creature in this wood.
Just walk behind me and soon you'll see,
Everyone is afraid of me."

"*All right,*" said the Gruffalo, bursting with laughter.
"*You go ahead and I'll follow after.*"

They walked and walked till the Gruffalo said,
"*I hear a hiss in the leaves ahead.*"

"It's Snake," said the mouse. "Why, Snake, hello!"
Snake took one look at the Gruffalo.
"Oh crumbs!" he said, *"Goodbye, little mouse,"*
And off he slid to his logpile house.

"You see?" said the mouse. "I told you so."
"Amazing!" said the Gruffalo.

They walked some more till the Gruffalo said,
"I hear a hoot in the trees ahead."

"It's Owl," said the mouse. "Why, Owl, hello!"
Owl took one look at the Gruffalo.
"*Oh dear!*" he said, "*Goodbye, little mouse,*"
And off he flew to his treetop house.

"You see?" said the mouse. "I told you so."
"*Astounding!*" said the Gruffalo.

They walked some more till the Gruffalo said,
"*I can hear feet on the path ahead.*"

"It's Fox," said the mouse. "Why, Fox, hello!"
Fox took one look at the Gruffalo.
"Oh help!" he said, *"Goodbye, little mouse,"*
And off he ran to his underground house.

"Well, Gruffalo," said the mouse. "You see?
Everyone is afraid of me!
But now my tummy's beginning to rumble.
My favourite food is — gruffalo crumble!"

"*Gruffalo crumble!*" the Gruffalo said,
And quick as the wind he turned and fled.